Read the Green words

For each word ask your child to read the separate sounds, e.g. 'r-e-d', 'a-w-ay' and then blend sounds together to make the word, e.g. 'red', 'away'. Sometimes one sound is represented by more than one letter, e.g. 'ng', 'ay', 'ck'. These are underlined.

day   hay   away   play   stay   that

thing   long   hatch

Ask your child to read the word in syllables.

drag` on → dragon

mass` ive → massive

Ask your child to read the root word first and then the word with the ending.

rock → rocks   crack → cracking

sunn` y → sunny

Read the Red words (*red for this book only)

Red words don't sound like they look. Read the words out to your child. Explain that he or she will have to stop and think about how to say the red words in the story.

ago   flew*   she   the   laid*   of   one

story*   I   hear*

Dragon bay

Introduction

Have you ever seen an egg hatch?
In this story some children are told a tale about a dragon's
egg but they don't believe it's true!
Do you think dragons might really exist?

Long ago, on a sunny day,

a big red dragon flew this
way.

She hid in the rocks in Dragon Bay,

and laid an egg on a nest
of hay.

She hid the egg and went away.

But . . . that dragon's egg
may hatch one day!

Oh, that's just a story, let's stay and play.

Help! Is that a tap, tap, tapping?

And this big rock is crack, crack, **cracking**!

It isn't a rock . . . it's a massive egg!

And that thing in the crack
is . . . a dragon's leg!

Help! Run away!

Questions to talk about

Ask your child:

Page 9: *Where did the dragon lay an egg?*

Page 10: Why do you think the dragon put the egg on the rocks?

Page 12: What did the children want to do after the story?

Page 19: Which part of the baby dragon came out of the egg first?

Speed words

Ask your child to read the words across the rows, down the columns and in and out of order, clearly and quickly.

play	egg	dragon	crack	help
the	rock	can	hatch	bay
nest	long	way	big	and
red	stay	just	hid	leg